To the memory of my grandmother, who worked in a shirtwaist
factory at the same time Rivka's mother did
—L.W.

To the right to experience the first day of school
—A.L.

Library of Congress Cataloging-in-Publication Data is available upon request.
ISBN 978-0-593-48207-0 (trade) — ISBN 978-0-593-48208-7 (lib. bdg.)
ISBN 978-0-593-48209-4 (ebook)

The artist used gouache and colored pencil along with
digital tools to create the illustrations for this book.
The text of this book is set in 14-point Archer.
Interior design by Rachael Cole

MANUFACTURED IN CHINA
10 9 8 7 6 5 4 3 2 1
First Edition

RIVKA'S PRESENTS

Words by **Laurie Wallmark** Images by **Adelina Lirius**

RANDOM HOUSE STUDIO NEW YORK

Rivka waved out the window to the iceman. "Today's my first day of school!"

Mama lowered her sewing. "Oh, Rivka,
I thought you understood. You can't go to
school right now."

Rivka stopped waving and went to Mama.
"But why, Mama?"

"Papa is very sick with the flu and
can't work.

"Starting tomorrow, I have to work at the shirtwaist factory, so I need you to mind little Miriam. When Papa is better, you can go to school."

Rivka's eyes teared up. "Yes, Mama."

Mama nodded and returned to her sewing.

Rivka raced out of the apartment, down two flights of stairs, and out the door.

Wham! Rivka crashed into the grocery-shop easel on the sidewalk.
She picked up the stand. "I'm sorry, Mr. Solomon."

"No harm done."

Rivka stared at the lines and curves on his slate. "Mr. Solomon,
can you teach me to write?"

"I'm sorry, bubbeleh." He swept the sidewalk. "I am much too busy."

"I can help you."

"Help me? A tiny little thing like you?"

"I can wash your windows." Rivka looked at Mr. Solomon's broom. "And sweep."

"Hmmm. Work for lessons?"

"Yes, but I need to bring Miriam. Is that all right?"

Mr. Solomon stroked his beard. "Agreed."

The next morning, Rivka swept the floorboards and wiped the counter.

She washed the window and stacked potatoes. While Rivka worked, she sang to her baby sister.

"All done?"

Mr. Solomon checked his pocket watch.

"Plenty of time for your first lesson."

"This is an A." Rivka took the chalk and drew a shaky letter A. Then another. And another.

"Good, good." Mr. Solomon gave her an apple. "A is for apple, to share with your sister."

Every morning, Rivka swept and cleaned and stacked and learned her ABCs.

By the time the trees were losing
their leaves, Rivka could sound out
the labels on Mama's preserves.
But Papa was still sick in bed.

On Mondays in the fall, Rivka brought Mama's piecework to Mr. Cohen, the tailor. He checked the shirtsleeves and made a mark on his paper.

"What are you writing?" Rivka asked.

"Numbers."

Rivka looked at the squiggles. "Mr. Cohen, can you teach me to add numbers?"

He glanced up from his paper. "Well . . ."

"I can help you. I can make deliveries."

He nodded. "Agreed."

Rivka came back the next week, and Mr. Cohen piled shirts in the wagon.

Rivka pulled the heavy cart along the cobblestone streets. She sang in time to the rattle of the wheels. As she passed the school, Rivka looked at the children in class. She sighed and continued on.

When she returned, Mr. Cohen placed a button on the stoop. "First lesson. One."

Rivka touched the button. "One."

He slid two more buttons forward. "Add two."

"Two, three."

By the time the snow flurries were swirling, Rivka could add pennies for Mama to pay the iceman.

But Papa was still sick.

Every Friday in the winter, before the Sabbath, Mama sent Rivka across the hall to clean for their elderly neighbor, Mrs. Langholtz. Rivka dusted and scrubbed and sang to Miriam.

The sweet smell of baking challah filled the apartment. While Rivka cleaned, Mrs. Langholtz picked up her book.

"What are you reading?" Rivka asked.

"The history of my new country. I am studying to become a citizen."

"Can you teach me about America?"

Mrs. Langholtz chuckled. "I do not think I know enough."

"I can help you. I'll listen to you recite."

"A wonderful idea. Such a shayna maideleh." Mrs. Langholtz patted Rivka's cheek. "Agreed."

When Rivka finished her cleaning, Mrs. Langholtz said, "For your first lesson, I will share what I learned today. In America, we do not have a king."

By the time the flowers were blooming, Rivka knew the names of the forty-eight states and could sing all four verses of "My Country, 'Tis of Thee."

Papa was still sick but could now join the family at the dinner table.

One afternoon in the spring, Mama sent Rivka to buy a spool of thread. When she returned, the parlor was filled with people.

"Surprise!" Mr. Solomon said.

"Mazel tov!" Mrs. Langholtz said.

"Congratulations!" Mr. Cohen said.

"Mama, Papa, why is everyone here?"

"It's a party," Mama said. "For you and your teachers."

"But how . . . how do you know about my lessons?"

Mama winked. "A mama knows."

Mrs. Langholtz cut the first slice of honey cake. "For Rivka, because learning should always be sweet."

Mr. Cohen held up a blouse. "A shirtwaist. For school."

Mr. Solomon gave Rivka a pen and a bottle of ink.

"A scholar needs proper tools."

Rivka beamed. "Thank you, everyone."

"Mama and I have a surprise for you, too," Papa said.
"I am no longer sick."

Rivka hugged Papa. "That's the best present of all."

Mama's eyes twinkled. "So . . ."

Rivka clapped her hands. "Tomorrow's my first day of school!"

AUTHOR'S NOTE
New York City, 1918, Life on the Lower East Side

Rivka and her family are not real people, but their story is based on the living and working situations common to many immigrants. Like many of their neighbors, Rivka's parents were born in another country. In search of a better life, immigrants came to the United States from Russia, Poland, Germany, Italy, and many other places. They had heard that in America, the streets were paved with gold. Hopeful immigrants called the United States the Goldene Medina, the Golden Country.

Many families lived in five- or six-story tenement buildings that didn't have an elevator. Nearly all the apartments had only three tiny rooms—a kitchen, a parlor, and a bedroom without a door. Children like Rivka and Miriam slept together in the same bed. In larger families, some people had to sleep in the parlor. The family shared a bathroom with the other families on the floor. On bath day, the mother heated bathwater on her coal-burning stove.

With only one or two windows to let in fresh air, summers were hot and muggy. Neighbors often agreed to leave their doors open to get a cross-breeze between apartments. During the winter, the cast-iron stove in the kitchen provided the only heat.

Because of the crowded living conditions, diseases spread rapidly. Tuberculosis and influenza were common. A simple cough could lead to a serious illness, even death.

In 1918, a global flu pandemic hit the United States. The deadly virus took tens of millions of lives around the world. Like Rivka's papa, some people were lucky enough to recover. But, also like Papa, people often took many months to be strong enough to work again. And some, like Mama and the girls, were fortunate to never fall ill.

Times were hard for families like Rivka's. Sometimes parents had to go without food so the children would have enough to eat. Even so, there were nights when children like Rivka and Miriam went to bed hungry.

Education was the best way to get a good job and escape poverty. Unfortunately, many children had to work and couldn't go to school. Few stayed in school past the eighth grade. In spite of these difficulties, enterprising children could sometimes find ways to learn.

Just like Rivka.

GLOSSARY

English Words

challah—egg bread made from braided dough; eaten on the Sabbath and holidays

piecework—sewing done at home and paid for by the piece instead of by the hour

Sabbath—day of rest and religious observance; for Jews, it lasts from sundown Friday to nightfall Saturday

shirtwaist—tailored blouse

stoop—short staircase at the entrance of a city building

tenement—apartment building

Yiddish Words*

bubbeleh—darling

Goldene Medina—Golden Country

mazel tov—congratulations

shayna maideleh—pretty little girl

* Yiddish was the language spoken by most Jewish immigrants from Eastern Europe, and it is still spoken by many Jewish people today.